JOSEFINA

JEANETTE WINTER

Harcourt Brace & Company

SAN DIEGO NEW YORK LONDON

This story was inspired by Josefina Aguilar,
a beloved Mexican folk artist who is still creating
her painted clay figures in the village of Ocotlán today.

Requests for permission to make copies of any part of the work should
be mailed to: Permissions Department, Harcourt Brace & Company,
6277 Sea Harbor Drive, Orlando, Florida 32887-6777.

Library of Congress Cataloging-in-Publication Data
Winter, Jeanette.
Josefina/Jeanette Winter.
p.   cm.
Summary: A counting book inspired by Mexican folk artist
Josefina Aguilar who makes painted clay figures.
ISBN 0-15-201091-2
[1. Artists—Fiction. 2. Mexico—Fiction. 3. Counting.]
I. Title.
PZ7.W7547Jo   1996
[E]—dc20   95-34110

First edition

A C E F D B

Printed in Singapore

The illustrations in this book were done in acrylics
on Strathmore Bristol paper.
The display type and text type were set in Icone 55
by Thompson Type, San Diego, California.
Color separations by Bright Arts, Ltd., Singapore
Printed and bound by Tien Wah Press, Singapore
This book was printed with soya-based inks on Leykam recycled paper,
which contains more than 20 percent postconsumer waste
and has a total recycled content of at least 50 percent.
Production supervision by Warren Wallerstein and Pascha Gerlinger
Designed by Jeanette Winter and Kaelin Chappell

For Elisa

E veryone in Ocotlán knew the pink wall

where the painted clay figures watched from the fence.

Behind the wall, in the patio, Mama and Papa Aguilar
worked with the soft clay. Baby Josefina watched
as the little figures filled the patio.
When she was old enough, her tiny fingers worked
the clay, too.

Josefina watched as Papa filled the kiln with their figures, and Mama added the firewood. They waited for the clay to bake in the fire — seven long hours. Then Josefina painted her own little boys and girls and animals and birds.

She loved the clay.

The years went by.

Mama and Papa died,

but Josefina kept working with the clay.

She married José and kept working.

Their first baby was born,

and Josefina kept working.

Then another baby was born,

and Josefina kept working.

Another baby was born,

and another, and another,

until there were nine children.

And still Josefina kept working with the clay.

Every day she went to the patio.

José mixed the clay and the children helped paint

while Josefina made her world.

Early one morning before dawn,

Josefina made a sun to light the sky.

Then she made two angels

and gave them wings to fly up to the sky.

Josefina carved windows and doors in three clay houses,
to let the sun shine in.

CUATRO VENDEDORAS DE FLORES

And in the sunshine, flowers bloomed.

Josefina sniffed the sweet smell

and made four women to sell the blossoms.

5 CINCO CAMPESINOS **5**

In the heat of the day,

five farmers toiled in Josefina's sunny patio,

as they did in the fields in the valley.

SEIS MADRES Y SEIS BEBÉS

6 6

Josefina made six babies for six mamas to hold,

while she held her own dear baby close.

SIETE MARIACHIS 7 7

Oh, the music of the mariachis in the zócalo

made Josefina want to sing and dance!

Her seven musicians played

as the sun set in the sky.

In the twilight, Josefina remembered

Mama and Papa in heaven.

Eight mourners remembered with her

as she drew their tears with a thorn.

But life goes on.

Josefina laughed at her nine skeletons.

She was not afraid for night to fall.

In the darkness, Josefina made ten stars

to twinkle bright in the sky.

Ten stars shined on

nine skeletons who danced around

eight mourners who heard

seven mariachis who serenaded

six mamas and babies who waited for

five farmers who brought flowers to

four flower sellers who sold blossoms at

three houses.

Two angels kept watch as

the sun slowly rose in the sky.

Then Josefina slept.